SAMMY SPIDER'S
PASSOVER
FUN BOOK

Sylvia A. Rouss

Illustrated by
Katherine Janus Kahn

KAR-BEN
PUBLISHING

ABOUT PASSOVER

Passover celebrates the exodus of the Israelite slaves from Egypt and the birth of the Jewish people as a nation. The holiday, observed in late March or April, begins with a festive meal called a *seder*. Families gather to read the *Haggadah*, a book which tells the story of the Jewish people's historic journey to freedom. The seder follows a special order. Children are involved in asking questions about the rituals and in searching for a hidden *matzah* called the *afikomen*. Symbolic foods recall the bitterness of slavery, the haste in which the Jews left, and the joy of freedom. During the holiday week no *hametz* (leavened food, such as bread) is eaten. *Matzah,* a flat cracker, takes the place of bread.

Text copyright © 2002 by Sylvia A. Rouss
Illustrations copyright © 2002 by Katherine Janus Kahn

ISBN-13: 978–1–58013–033–2
ISBN-10: 1–58013–033–X

KAR-BEN PUBLISHING
A division of Lerner Publishing Group, Inc.
241 First Avenue North
Minneapolis, MN 55401 USA
800-4KARBEN
www.karben.com

Manufactured in the United States Of America
6 – DOC – 9/1/14

Sammy listens to all the birds sing,
"Passover is coming, for now it is spring."
Eight little birds. Where can they be?
Can you find them hidden in this tree?

Find and circle the 8 birds, a squirrel, and Sammy, too.
Then color the picture.

Josh is sweeping up crumbs with his broom.
Can you find the hametz* that's left in this room?

Circle the items that don't belong.

Foods that are not eaten on Passover

These cards will help you invite
Your special friends to seder night.

Make copies of these cards, color them, and send to your seder guests.

Name: _____
Place: _____
_____
Date: _____
Time: _____

Name: _____
Place: _____
_____
Date: _____
Time: _____

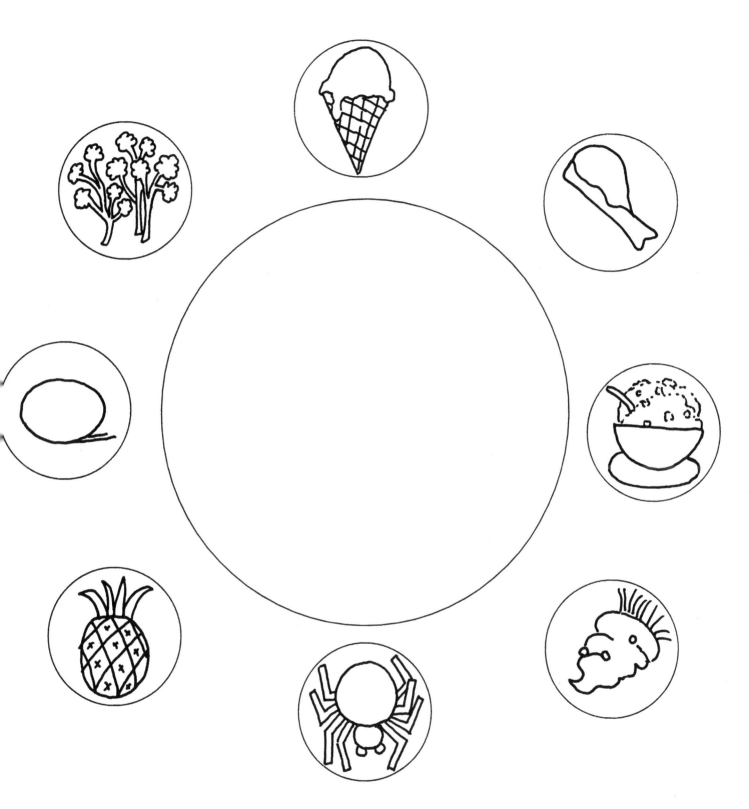

Passover is coming! Josh can't wait.
Help him fill the seder plate.

Copy the five objects that belong onto the seder plate:
bone, egg, charoset, parsley, maror

Preparing for seder can be fun.
Complete each job and you'll be done.

See game instructions on following page.

Game instructions (for two players):

Cut out game cards and give each player one set. Use buttons as markers. The youngest goes first. Each player flips a coin and moves ahead one space for heads, two spaces for tails. When a player lands on a picture square, he or she collects the corresponding picture card. Continue around the board until one player has collected all eight cards. You will probably have to go around the board more than once.

Note: You may want to copy or paste the cards onto heavier paper and cover with plastic adhesive. You can also play matching and memory games with these cards.

CHANGE DISHES	MATZAH	SET TABLE	ELIJAH'S CUP
HAGGADAH	SEDER PLATE	PILLOW	CLEAN HOUSE
CHANGE DISHES	MATZAH	SET TABLE	ELIJAH'S CUP
HAGGADAH	SEDER PLATE	PILLOW	CLEAN HOUSE

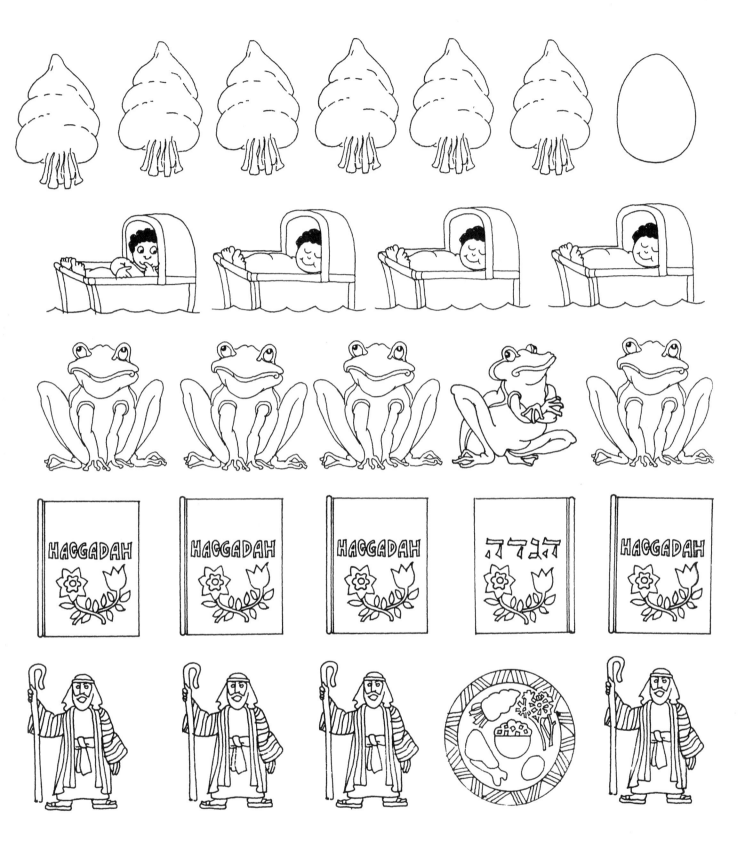

Help Sammy play this seder game.
Circle the one that's not the same.

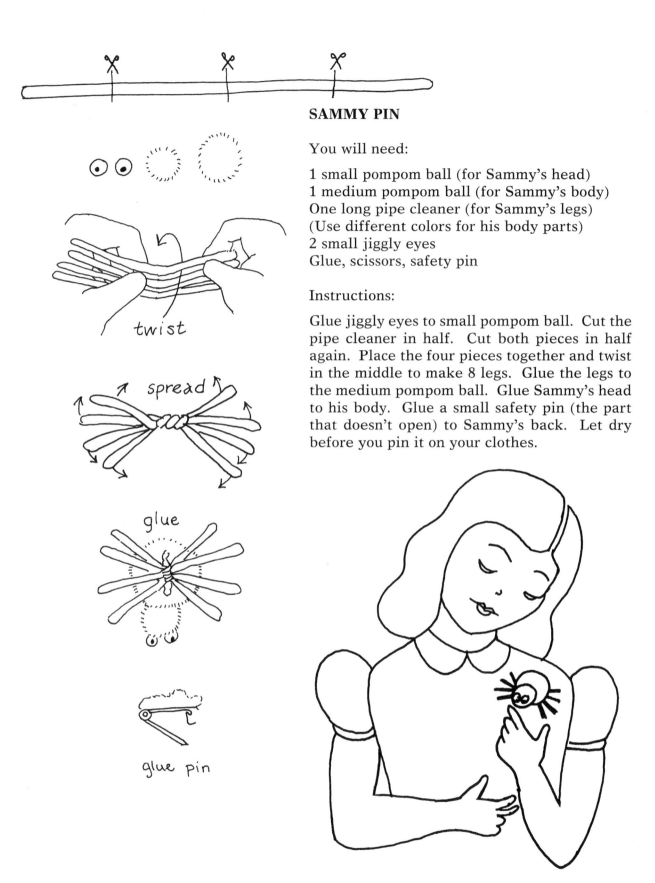

SAMMY PIN

You will need:

1 small pompom ball (for Sammy's head)
1 medium pompom ball (for Sammy's body)
One long pipe cleaner (for Sammy's legs)
(Use different colors for his body parts)
2 small jiggly eyes
Glue, scissors, safety pin

Instructions:

Glue jiggly eyes to small pompom ball. Cut the pipe cleaner in half. Cut both pieces in half again. Place the four pieces together and twist in the middle to make 8 legs. Glue the legs to the medium pompom ball. Glue Sammy's head to his body. Glue a small safety pin (the part that doesn't open) to Sammy's back. Let dry before you pin it on your clothes.

twist

spread

glue

glue pin

Make this Sammy pin and later
You can wear it to the seder.

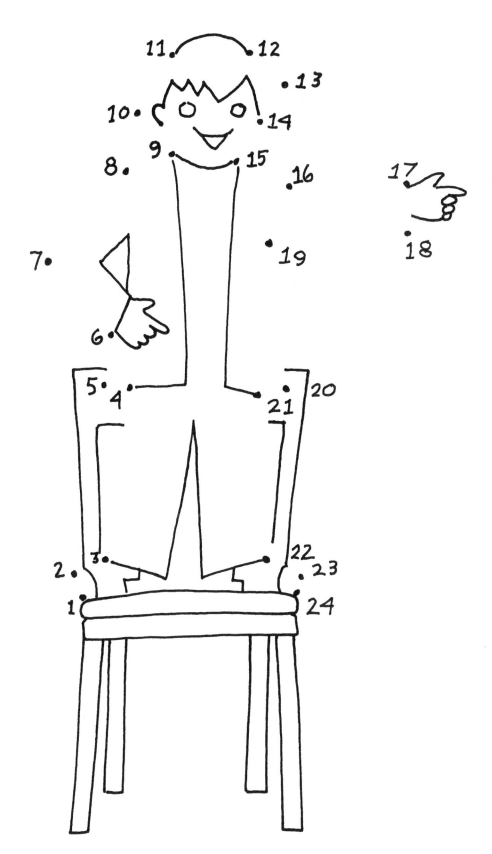

Who is asking the Four Questions tonight?
Connect the dots to see if you are right!

Who was the hero of the Exodus?
Sammy is sure that you can guess
If you unscramble the letters S O M E S.

Then color the areas that have these letters to discover a hidden picture.

The Jewish people want to be free.
Show them the way to cross the Red Sea.

These two seders look the same.
Find out what's different to play this game.

Can you find at least 10 things that are different?

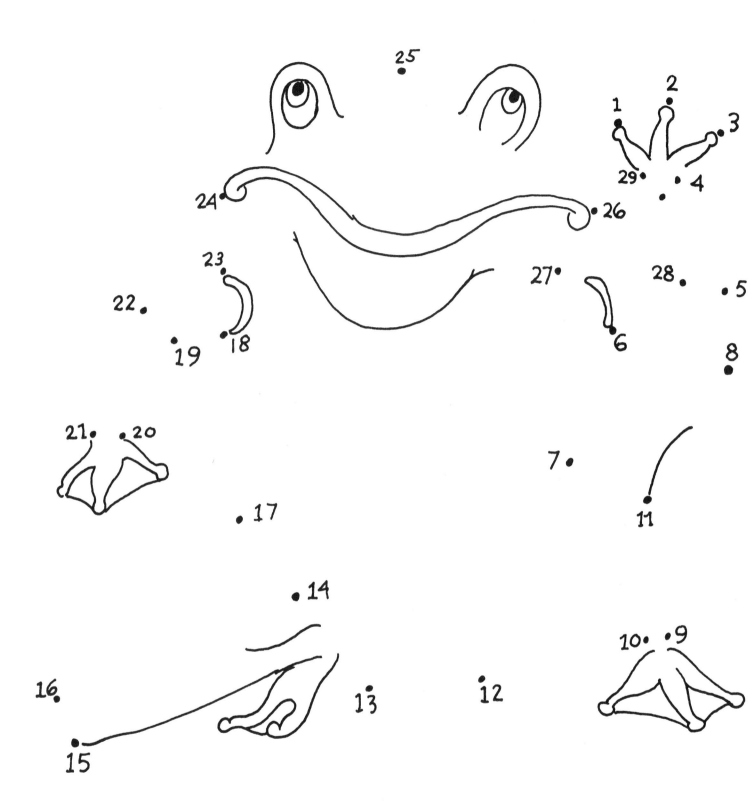

One morning Pharaoh woke in his bed.
Which plague was crawling all over his head?

Connect the dots.

Word puzzles are a lot of fun.
Sammy is sure you can solve this one.

```
H  T  S  E  T  R  Y  J  L
A  G  H  R  E  G  G  S  O
G  P  A  S  S  O  V  E  R
G  M  N  S  O  I  L  D  M
A  O  K  A  R  S  Z  E  A
D  S  B  M  A  R  O  R  T
A  E  O  M  H  S  O  J  Z
H  S  N  Y  C  A  G  D  A
Q  Y  E  L  S  R  A  P  H
```

Look up, down, forward, and backward.
Find and circle these words:

PASSOVER	CHAROSET
MAROR	HAGGADAH
JOSH	SHANKBONE
PARSLEY	SAMMY
MATZAH	SEDER
EGG	MOSES

Finding the afikomen is a chore
But Sammy's found it and lots more!

Find and circle these hidden objects: afikomen, frog,
Kiddush cup, seder plate, candlesticks, Sammy Spider

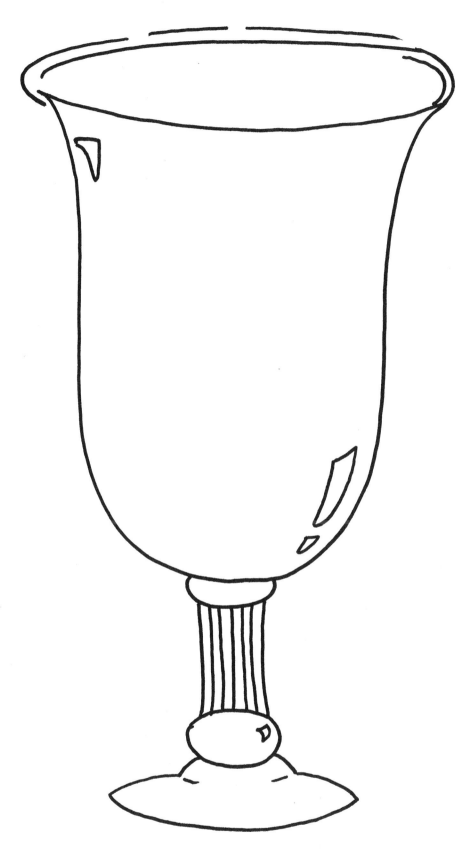

Elijah's coming, here's his cup,
Will he drink the wine all up?

Decorate Elijah's cup.

SPIDER WEB MATZAH

Ingredients:

1/2 c. chocolate chips
1 teaspoon margarine
1 matzah

Instructions:

Melt chocolate and margarine over low heat. Place matzah on a plate. Dip a teaspoon into the melted mixture and drizzle over the matzah to create a spider web pattern. Use a raisin to put Sammy in the web. Allow to cool before eating.

Here's a special Passover treat.
A spider web that you can eat!

$4.95 USA

Join Sammy Spider in his many adventures during Passover! Puzzles, mazes, crafts, games, and more will entertain children as they learn about the holiday with this lovable spider and his friend Josh.

Do you have these best-selling SAMMY SPIDER books?

Sammy Spider's First Day of School

Sammy Spider's First Haggadah

Sammy Spider's First Hanukkah

Sammy Spider's First Mitzvah

Sammy Spider's First Passover

Sammy Spider's First Purim

Sammy Spider's First Rosh Hashanah

Sammy Spider's First Shabbat

Sammy Spider's First Shavuot

Sammy Spider's First Simchat Torah

Sammy Spider's First Sukkot

Sammy Spider's First Trip to Israel

Sammy Spider's First Tu B'Shevat

Sammy Spider's First Yom Kippur

Sammy Spider's Hanukkah Fun Book

Sammy Spider's Israel Fun Book

Sammy Spider's New Friend

Sammy Spider's Passover Fun Book

Sammy Spider's Shabbat Fun Book

SAMMY SPIDER PLUSH TOY now available!

KAR-BEN
PUBLISHING
www.karben.com
800-4KARBEN

ISBN 978-1-58013-033-2

50495

9 781580 130332

Se ifting for the Viola

by Cassia Harvey

C. Harvey Publications